Crestwood Park can be a scary place . . .

"I saw it again," Berrie whispered into the phone. "The gray dog. The one that looks like the coyote."

"When?" asked Tara. "Where?"

Berrie looked around. Grandma and her parents and her aunt and uncle were in the living room. They were talking so loudly they couldn't hear her in the hall.

"After you left," she said in a low voice. "The same place we fed the squirrels. First I saw the dog just standing there, like it was frozen. Then it ran right toward me! But it wasn't after me!"

The CREATURE in CRESTWOOD PARK

BY BARBARA FORD

ILLUSTRATED BY DAN ANDREASEN

little rainbow®
Troll

For Patsy,
who saw the creature with me.
—B. F.

CHAPTER 1

"We saw this alligator 20 feet long!" Berrie Lockwood breathed into the phone. "And then it started chasing us!"

Her best friend Tara gasped. "So what did you do?"

"We rode our bikes as fast as we could. I could hear it!"

"Then what happened?"

Berrie's mother had come to the kitchen doorway. Berrie turned her back. She brought the phone close to her mouth.

"It opened its mouth with all these teeth, then closed it—*click!*" Berrie brought her upper teeth down on her lower teeth.

"It couldn't catch us, though. We rode too fast," she added.

"I wish I had gone to Florida for spring vacation," said Tara. "Nothing interesting ever happens around here."

"Berrie, would you please set the table?" called her mother.

"Got to go," said Berrie. "See you tomorrow. In school." Tara groaned.

Berrie groaned, too. Tomorrow was Monday, the first day after spring vacation.

In the kitchen, Berrie took silverware out of the drawer and napkins out of the holder.

"Berrie, what's that I heard about a 20–foot alligator?" asked Mrs. Lockwood. "The ranger told us the biggest ones in Florida today are 12 feet."

Berrie flew into the dining room. She put a knife, fork, spoon and napkin at four places. Then she walked slowly back to the kitchen.

"And we weren't chased by an alligator," her mother said. "Why, all those 'gators we saw were asleep."

"One moved! I saw it!" Berrie moved the stool below the cupboard. She took down four glasses. In her mind, a long gray-green creature rose up on four short, fat legs. It waddled forward, its long tail dragging.

The kitchen door opened. Mr. Lockwood and Jill, Berrie's sister, came in.

"Well, it sounds like you're telling stories again," said Mrs. Lockwood.

"What's this about stories?" asked Mr. Lockwood.

"Berrie told Tara we were chased by a 20–foot alligator," said Mrs. Lockwood.

"Twenty feet!" Jill bent over, laughing. "They weren't even half that long! Anyway, they were all sleeping."

"A big one got up!" cried Berrie. "I saw it! I saw it when you guys were looking the other way!"

"Yeah, right," said Jill.

"Mmmmmm," said Mr. Lockwood, changing the subject. "It smells like fried chicken."

"It is," said Mrs. Lockwood. "And it's ready. Take this bowl. Jill, the salad. Berrie, the rolls."

When everything was on the table, they all sat down.

"It did move," said Berrie. She looked around the table. Her mother was frowning. Jill was rolling her eyes. And her father was shaking his head.

"Stick to the facts," he said. "That's a good rule, Berrie." He passed her the platter of chicken.

The facts, thought Berrie as she took a drumstick. In her mind, the long, gray-green animal opened its long jaw. Inside were hundreds of teeth. *Crunch!* The jaw closed on a bicycle.

It could have happened! Even if it didn't. She sighed. The facts were so boring.

CHAPTER 2

"I have a special assignment for the class," Mrs. Brindle was saying. "Write this in your notebooks."

Berrie held her pencil over her writing notebook.

"My favorite wild animal," said Mrs. Brindle.

My favorite wild animal, wrote Berrie. Then she printed ALLIGATOR in big letters. She knew how to spell it because she read about alligators when she was in Florida. The alligator was so long. Of course the giraffe was nice, too. It was so high. How did you spell "giraffe"? She printed GIRAF in big letters. But an elephant would be good, too. Elephants were bigger than anything. ELEFANT, Berrie wrote.

"But you must write about an animal that lives in this state," said Mrs. Brindle. She looked around the classroom. "And that you have seen *personally*."

Berrie sat back in her chair, feeling disappointed. There were no interesting animals in their state at all. Then a thought jumped into her mind. She waved her hand.

"Mrs. Brindle! What if an animal lives in the zoo in this state?"

"Zoos don't count. You must have seen your animal in the wild. But don't just tell me what you saw. Read about your animal. You'll have a whole month to complete your assignment. Tell me what animal you've chosen by next Monday."

Berrie drew a picture of an alligator in her notebook. There weren't any wild animals near them. They lived in the city. The closest thing to the wild was Crestwood Park. It was

big, but it had busy streets on all four sides. The biggest wild animal in Crestwood Park was probably a squirrel.

Berrie printed SQUIRELL in big letters. She looked at the word and frowned. Then she crossed it out.

"We'll read our assignments aloud in class," said Mrs. Brindle. "Then we'll vote on the best one."

"Will there be a prize?" asked Jeff, waving his hand.

"Certainly," said Mrs. Brindle with a smile.

After school, Berrie and Tara walked home together, the way they did every day.

"I'm writing about the rabbit," said Tara. "I saw some in Crestwood Park."

"Rabbits?" Berrie said disdainfully.

"Rabbits are cute," said Tara. "I like their little white tails."

"Sure," said Berrie, thinking that rabbits were boring. All they did was hop, hop, hop. "If we lived in Florida, I could write about alligators," she said. "Or sharks!"

They were passing Crestwood Park. A pigeon walked across the sidewalk.

"If we lived in Maine, I could write about the moose," said Berrie. "Last summer I saw a moose in Maine. It had these huge horns. It ran after our car!"

"Really?"

Berrie nodded. "But my father went fast and we got away. It was close."

"You didn't say it chased you before," observed Tara. "You just said you saw a moose."

"Well, it did." said Berrie. In her mind, the moose with the huge horns lowered its head and moved toward the car. It could have been running after them. The ranger told them a moose butted a car in the park once.

"Hey!" Jeff and Matt walked by them. "Guess what animal I'm going to write about," said Jeff.

"The cockroach," said Berrie. Jeff lived in an apartment house on Tara's street. Last summer his parents had to fog to get rid of the cockroaches.

Jeff yanked Berrie's ponytail. He danced out of reach of Berrie's arm. "The bear!" he yelled.

"There aren't any bears in this state, Jeff!"

"Are so! They're in this one little corner, in the mountains. We went there last summer and I saw a bear crossing the road."

"I'm doing the deer, " said Matt. "I saw them in the state park."

Berrie watched Jeff and Matt move off ahead of them. The bear! Nobody else would write about anything as interesting as the bear. Jeff would win the prize. Unless . . .

"What are you going to write about?" asked Tara.

"Something . . . interesting," said Berrie, nodding thoughtfully. "Something . . . different." She could see herself standing in front of the room, reading her assignment. Everyone would clap. Mrs. Brindle would nod the way she did when she was pleased.

Maybe she would win the prize!

She needed information on animals. Lots of information. The big library downtown had lots of books. Maybe if she looked at those books, she'd find an interesting animal. A different animal. An animal she'd seen.

"Tomorrow I'm going to the big library to find an animal," said Berrie. "Want to go?"

"Yes!" said Tara.

CHAPTER 3

Plop! A drop fell on Berrie's head. Putting her head down, she turned her bike to cut through Crestwood Park to Tara's house. It was so early and so cloudy that there was practically nobody else in the park.

The rain was coming down faster now, but the leaves on the big trees caught lots of the drops. Berrie pedaled swiftly up the car road. Ahead she could see the fountain. Even the old lady who fed pigeons wasn't there.

Suddenly a squirrel dashed across Berrie's path. Berrie hit her brakes so hard that the bike skidded on the wet pavement.

Crash! The bike was lying on the road and so was she.

Berrie wasn't hurt but she was all muddy. Berrie sat up, feeling indignant.

"Hey, squirrel!" she called. "Dumb squirrel! You made me fall, you know that?"

She was not going to write about squirrels, that was for sure!

Just then a dog appeared from out of nowhere. It was a middle-sized dog, with thick gray fur mixed with white and black. The dog's big ears stood straight up, but its tail hung low. The dog ran right by Berrie, moving very fast. It looked neither to the right nor the left.

"Hey, dog!" she called, but the yellow eyes in the long, thin face stared straight ahead.

Berrie looked around. There was nobody in sight. Maybe the dog was lost.

But it didn't look lost. It was running past the fountain now. It ran in a line so straight it was like it was following a line painted on the ground. Where was it going? Wherever it was, the dog was going there as fast as it could.

The dog disappeared into the trees beyond the fountain.

Berrie wiped some of the mud off her jeans with her hands. Uh-oh. There was a hole in her new jeans. Great! "Dumb squirrel!" she shouted again as she picked up her bike.

Tara's apartment building was only a few blocks from the far end of the park. After ringing the doorbell, Berrie waited to be buzzed through the big front door. She had thought she wasn't hurt, but now her knee was aching. When the door opened, she wheeled her bike into the lobby. Tara lived on the first floor.

Tara opened the door. She looked Berrie up and down. "What happened to you?"

"This dumb squirrel ran across the park road right in front of me! I put on my brakes and the bike skidded. There's a hole in my new jeans. And now my knee hurts." Berrie parked the bike in the hall. She limped into the apartment.

Tara gave her an ice pack out of the refrigerator to put on her knee. Soon it hurt less.

"You can iron on a jeans patch to cover the hole," said Tara helpfully.

"I guess," Berrie sighed. Her new jeans would never look the same. And all because of a squirrel!

A few minutes later the two girls got on the bus at the corner. The bus drove down the whole length of Crestwood Park before it turned. Berrie searched the park with her eyes. No sign of the dog. What kind of dog was it, anyway? She had never seen a dog like that. It must be some kind of mixed breed, Berrie thought. Jasper, her dog, was a mixed breed.

When they got to the library, the librarian told them where the animal books were. They walked up and down the stacks.

"Look!" whispered Tara. "Three books about rabbits!"

Then Berrie found a big book called *Mammals of North America*. A lot of mammals, she knew, had soft fur. She liked animals with fur the best.

They carried their books to a big table. In

Berrie's book, the animals were in alphabetical order. Elephant was under *E*. ELEPHANT. She'd spelled it wrong. She turned to *G*. GIRAFFE. She'd spelled that wrong, too. If only she could write about a cool animal like the giraffe or the elephant—then she'd definitely win the prize.

Maybe she ought to start at the *A*s. She flipped through the shiny pages. Armadillos. They had those in Florida, too. But not here. Bears. That reminded Berrie of Jeff. She flipped faster, determined to find a great animal. Caribou. Coyotes . . .

Berrie gasped.

"What is it?" asked Tara.

Berrie pointed at the picture. The animal had gray and white and black fur, big ears that stood straight up, a long, pointed face, and yellow eyes. The yellow eyes stared up at Berrie. It was just like the dog she'd seen in the park.

"It wasn't a dog," she said. "It was a coyote!"

CHAPTER
4

Berrie and Tara stared at the picture in the book.

"It looked just like this coyote," said Berrie.

"But coyotes don't live around here," said Tara. "This is the city."

"I saw it! It looked just like the picture!" Berrie insisted.

Berrie and Tara checked out their books and left the library. As they rode the bus home, Tara turned the pages of one of her books. "Female rabbits are bigger than males," she read.

"Huh!" said Berrie. "Well, the coyote . . ." She turned to the part of her book about coyotes. "Coyotes are *a-dapt-a-ble* and intelligent," she read. She looked at Tara. "The coyote is lots smarter than the rabbit. I wouldn't write about the rabbit."

"Well, I've *seen* rabbits," said Tara. "Lots of them. You've never even seen a coyote."

"I did!"

"You didn't!"

Tara didn't believe her! Her best friend! If she didn't have to get her bike, she would have gotten right off the bus and gone home. She would never go anywhere with Tara again. But all she could do now was turn away from Tara and look out the window. They were passing the park again. She had seen it! And it was a coyote!

When the bus stopped at Tara's corner, they got off in silence. They walked down the street to Tara's apartment house in silence. They went down the hall in silence.

Tara opened her apartment door with her key. The door banged loudly behind her.

Berrie put the book on North American

mammals in her bike basket and wheeled her bike back down the hall. She had seen a coyote this morning, in Crestwood Park. And she would go back there right now and see it again.

She turned into the park through the big wrought iron gates. At this end of the park, there was a tall, narrow house with a tower on one side. That was where the park director had his office. She rode slowly along the car road. There were lots of people in the park now, because the sun was out.

Some people were eating their lunch in one of the picnic shelters. Berrie licked her lips. She was so hungry. But she had to look for the dog.

She turned the bike off the car road and rode down one of the paths. Crestwood Park was narrow, but it was long. She passed the tennis courts. She passed the pond. She passed the playground, the bandshell, and the picnic shelters. She passed the fountain, where the old lady was feeding pigeons.

There was a crowd of pigeons around her.

She speeded up again. Lots of people were walking dogs. But there was no sign of a dog with black, white, and gray fur, big ears that stood up, yellow eyes and a long, thin face. Berrie's stomach growled. She turned her bike back onto the car road. She rode back past the fountain, the picnic shelters, the bandshell, the playground, the pond, and the tennis courts. Still no gray dog.

"I'll find it!" she mumbled as she opened the door to her house. "I know it's here. Someplace."

Berrie's mom and dad were out shopping, but Jasper came out from under a table and wagged hello. Jill sat in a chair reading.

"I saw a coyote in Crestwood Park this morning!" said Berrie, petting Jasper's soft head.

"Coyotes don't live around here," said Jill, turning a page of her magazine.

"It looked exactly like the coyote in this book!" said Berrie, putting the big book on the

table. She turned the pages. "See?" She pointed to the picture of the gray, black, and white animal with the yellow eyes and the big ears that stood up and the long, pointed face.

Jill looked. "Coyotes like that don't live around here," she said. "We're in the *city*."

"But it was there! In the park! This morning! And there wasn't anybody with it!"

"It must have been a lost dog," said Jill, turning another page.

"It didn't act like a dog!"

Berrie looked down at Jasper. His old, brown eyes looked up at her. In her mind, she saw the gray dog moving quickly through the park. It looked neither to the right nor the left. The yellow eyes stared right through her. They were wild eyes, not dog eyes like Jasper's.

Jill turned another page of her magazine.

Berrie made herself a peanut butter and jelly sandwich. She decided not to tell her parents about the coyote. Her father would say she should stick to the facts. Her mother would just think she was telling stories again.

The face of the gray dog reappeared in her mind. The wild yellow eyes stared straight through her. She had seen it! She had! But how could she ever make anyone believe there was a coyote in Crestwood Park?

CHAPTER 5

"The raccoon," said Mrs. Brindle. "That's a good choice, Kelly. Where did you see the raccoon?"

"I saw it at my aunt's house in the country. We came home late at night and a raccoon was on top of the garbage can."

Mrs. Brindle wrote something in her big notebook.

Matt was waving his hand. "I'm going to write about deer," he said. "I saw them in the state park."

"Tara?" said Mrs. Brindle as Tara's hand waved.

Tara announced her choice of the rabbit.

The mallard duck, the red-tailed hawk, the groundhog, the skunk, the garter snake, and the box turtle were soon picked, too.

Jeff waved his hand. "I'm going to do the black bear," he said. I saw a black bear last summer in the mountains. It was walking across the road."

"I've heard there are a few black bears there," said Mrs. Brindle. "You're lucky to have seen one, Jeff. Now who hasn't chosen an animal? Berrie?"

Berrie took a deep breath. While she was listening to the other students, she had made up her mind. "I'm going to do the coyote." She looked at Tara out of the corner of her eye.

Tara was laughing!

"Berrie, you have to have seen this animal yourself," said Mrs. Brindle.

"I saw one on Saturday in Crestwood Park," said Berrie.

Everyone was laughing now.

"I did!" cried Berrie.

"Class," said Mrs. Brindle, holding up a

hand. "Berrie, this isn't a creative writing assignment. We do not want to make up seeing an animal. In this assignment we want to write about a real animal, such as the white-footed mouse. Perhaps you'd like to choose that animal. It's very common around here and I'm sure you've seen one."

Berrie scowled at Mrs. Brindle and shook her head.

"The crow?"

Berrie shook her head again.

"I know!" Mrs. Bridle smiled. "The squirrel. Nobody has picked that yet."

"I don't want to write about the squirrel!" cried Berrie.

Mrs. Brindle frowned. She tapped her pencil on the desk. "Berrie, I asked you to select an animal that you saw in this state. Since you haven't selected an appropriate animal, I am assigning you the squirrel." Mrs. Brindle wrote something in her notebook. "Now who else needs to choose an animal? Ashley?

Berrie slumped into her chair. An ordinary old squirrel that you could see any day! It was worse than the rabbit. And from the corner of her eye, she could see Tara trying not to laugh.

After school she walked home alone. She had seen the coyote. She knew it wasn't a dog. There was something wild about its eyes. There was something wild about the way it ran. She had never seen a dog that acted like that.

"Hey, Berrie! I bet you win the prize with the squirrel!"

Jeff yanked her ponytail as he went by. Matt was with him, and so was Tara. They were all laughing—laughing at her.

Berrie turned into the big wrought iron gates of Crestwood Park. She decided to go to the park and look for the coyote. She would look every single day until she found it.

CHAPTER
6

Every day that week was sunny and warm. Crestwood Park was full of people. Each day after school Berrie walked up the path on the Walker Street side of the park. She walked down the path on the King Street side. She looked in the playground and on tennis courts. She looked around the pond. She looked in every one of the picnic shelters. She looked around the fountain. She even looked in the yard of the house where the director had his office.

The gray dog wasn't in any of those places.

Berrie dropped to the ground next to a red picnic shelter. A squirrel came down a tree.

It sat on its hind legs, looking at her.

"Dumb squirrel!" said Berrie. She took out a cookie left over from lunch. She wouldn't give any to the squirrel. No, she would eat it all herself. She took a big bite.

The squirrel got down on all four legs and ran away.

When Berrie got home, Jill was standing at the kitchen counter cutting something. "You're late again," she said. "It's almost time for Mom to come home. Rinse the salad stuff."

Jill was in charge of meals, because she was three years older. Berrie took the lettuce out of the crisper and began pulling the leaves apart.

The front door opened. "Hi!" called Mrs. Lockwood's voice.

"See?" said Jill.

Berrie put the lettuce in the mesh basket to drip.

"Where do you go every day after school, anyway?" asked Jill.

Berrie couldn't tell Jill about looking for the gray dog—not after what she said. "I walk around Crestwood Park and look at the squirrels." she said. "It's for a school assignment."

After dinner, Berrie looked up squirrels in the book on North American mammals. There wasn't much exciting information about them. Then she turned to the *R*s and read about rabbits. When a rabbit was scared, it drummed on the ground with its hind feet. The back legs of rabbits were longer than the front legs. Some people ate rabbits.

Berrie wrinkled her nose. She wouldn't want to eat a rabbit. But rabbits were a lot more interesting than squirrels. How did she get stuck with the squirrel, anyway? Berrie frowned. The coyote, she remembered. That was why. And now it had disappeared.

On Sunday morning, Berrie dialed Tara's number. She hadn't talked to Tara all week.

Tara answered. She always answered, because she didn't have any brothers or sisters.

"It's me," said Berrie. "I read about the rabbit in my book. It's kind of interesting."

"I know. I'm going to talk about the cottontail rabbit. It's the one that lives around here."

"I got a book on squirrels in the library. There are lots of squirrels in Crestwood Park. Do you want to go to the park today and watch the squirrels and rabbits?"

"That sounds great!" said Tara.

They were friends again, thought Berrie as she hung up. It felt good to talk to Tara again. She skipped down the hall to her room. Besides the big book on North American mammals, there were two smaller books on the bed. One was about squirrels; the other was about coyotes.

Berrie picked up the coyote book. Then, with a sigh, she put it down, and picked up the book on squirrels instead.

CHAPTER
7

It was a little hot when Berrie and Tara got to the park on Sunday afternoon. They had brought a bag of popcorn to feed the squirrels and two carrots to feed the rabbits. The popcorn was good. Berrie looked at the bag. It was half gone.

"We've got to stop," said Berrie, folding the top of the popcorn bag over. "There won't be any left for the squirrels."

They walked slowly up the path, looking for squirrels and rabbits. They passed a red picnic shelter.

"When I was here before a squirrel came down that tree," said Berrie. "It wanted something to eat."

"Let's sit here, where we can watch for it," said Tara. She sat down on a bench facing the picnic shelter.

A boy rode by them and waved. It was Jeff. "Jeff's uncle is a biologist," said Tara. "He's telling him things about the black bear."

"Huh!" said Berrie, feeling cross. Jeff not only saw a bear, he had an uncle who was a biologist. And she had to write about the dumb squirrel.

Just then the girls saw something running through the low grass. Two squirrels stopped a little way from the bench. They sat up on their hind legs and looked at the girls.

"They're so cute!" said Tara.

Berrie opened the popcorn bag and reached inside. She threw some popcorn in the direction of the squirrels.

The squirrels found the popcorn in the grass. They sat on their hind legs and held the popcorn in their little paws. Their fluffy tails curved up in the air and then down, like question marks.

"They are kind of cute," said Berrie.

Berrie and Tara took turns throwing popcorn. The squirrels ate everything they threw. Then another squirrel came down a tree. It ate some popcorn, too.

"It's all gone," said Berrie. "Now let's look for rabbits."

The girls walked all the way up the path to the tennis courts. They saw more squirrels and pigeons. But they didn't see any rabbits.

"I saw rabbits in the park last fall," said Tara. "But I haven't seen any this year."

There was a long, low rumble from the sky.

"Thunder?" asked Tara.

More rumbles.

"Thunder," said Berrie, looking up through a hole in the tree branches. The sky, which had been so blue when they came to the park, was now dark gray.

The people on the tennis courts stopped playing and walked off the courts. The people in the picnic shelters packed up their food. Walking and running and riding bikes, people moved toward the park exits.

A streak of lightning split the gray sky.

"I'm going home!" cried Tara. "Do you want to come over?"

"I can't." Berrie shook her head. "Grandma's coming for dinner. Bye!"

Head down, Berrie trotted back through the park. By the time she got to the fountain, big drops had started to fall. There were so many leaves overhead that she didn't feel them at first. But then there were more and more drops, falling faster and faster through the leaves.

It was pouring! Her T-shirt was sopping wet. Berrie ran into the same red picnic shelter where she and Tara had fed the squirrels.

Overhead, the drops pounded on the top of the wooden shelter. Berrie squeezed some water out of her T-shirt and looked out at the rain. After a while the drops stopped pounding on the roof. They beat gently instead.

Berrie stuck her hand out of the shelter. The rain was letting up. There was nobody left in the park. Everyone had gone home.

Berrie noticed one of the squirrels run down a tree. It stopped to investigate something in the grass.

Then there was something to her left, something that hadn't been there before. She turned her head slowly. The gray dog stood there, one front leg raised. It stood so still it looked like one of the statues around the fountain.

Slowly, Berrie turned her head back. The squirrel was moving toward the picnic shelter, away from the tree. Out of the corner of her eye, she saw the gray dog spring into movement.

The squirrel dashed back to its tree, taking big jumps.

The dog flew past the shelter. It leaped into the air and landed with its front legs stretched out in front of it. With a toss of its head, it trotted past Berrie again. But this time there was something in its mouth. Something that had a tail. A long fluffy tail.

CHAPTER
8

"I saw it again," Berrie whispered into the phone. "The gray dog. The one that looks like the coyote."

"When?" asked Tara. "Where?"

Berrie looked around. Grandma and her parents and her aunt and uncle were in the living room. They were talking so loudly they couldn't hear her in the hall.

"After you left," she said in a low voice. "The same place we fed the squirrels. First I saw the dog just standing there, like it was frozen. Then it ran right toward me! But it wasn't after me!"

"Who was it after?"

"It jumped way up in the air. Then it came down and grabbed something with its two front paws. And after that I saw the squirrel's tail hanging out of its mouth!"

"It ate the squirrel!"

"Yes!"

There was silence on the phone. Then Tara said, "The squirrels were so cute."

"I know," said Berrie.

More silence. The squirrels were cute, thought Berrie. And the fluffy tail looked so sad hanging out of the dog's mouth. She had liked the gray dog before. But now she didn't. How could it eat a cute little animal like the squirrel?

"It must live in the park," said Tara at last.

"Yes. But where?" said Berrie.

"And why doesn't anybody see it?"

"I don't know."

"Hey, now you can write about the coyote!" said Tara. "You'll win the prize! All Jeff saw his bear do is walk across the road."

"But I've seen it when there's nobody else

around," said Berrie. "I don't think anybody will believe me."

"Yeah. Why does it come around when nobody's there?"

"I don't know. Anyway, I don't think I want to write about the coyote anymore. It's mean. It eats squirrels."

After Grandma left, Berrie ran back to her room. She picked up the book on squirrels, but then put it down. Then she picked up the book on coyotes and began to read.

"Rodents and rabbits lead the list of foods the coyote likes."

Rodents. Rats were rodents. So were mice. Were squirrels rodents?

Yes. Her dictionary said squirrels were rodents.

Berrie picked up the book on coyotes again. Rodents and rabbits. What had Tara said? There weren't any rabbits in Crestwood Park this year. Maybe the coyote ate them, too!

She read some more. "Coyotes are wary

of humans. They keep out of sight."

Berrie let the book drop to her bed. That's why she didn't see the gray dog when there were people around! Coyotes keep out of people's way. The one in the park only came out when there wasn't anybody around. All the pieces were fitting together like a puzzle. The gray dog *had* to be a coyote. A coyote that ate squirrels and rabbits. A coyote that kept out of sight when there were people around.

On Monday morning, Tara was waiting at the corner of the park. "I've found out a lot of things about coyotes," Berrie told her. "Their favorite food is rodents, and the squirrel is a rodent."

"And . . ." prompted Tara.

"They're shy around people. They keep out of sight!"

"That's why nobody else has seen it!"

"Yes!"

"It *is* a coyote!"

"I found out something else, too," said Berrie in a serious voice.

"What?"

"Their next favorite food is rabbits. Maybe that's why we didn't see any rabbits in the park."

Tara looked away. "Oh," she said.

They waited for the light at the corner of the park. There was a big map of the park next to the entrance. Berrie studied it.

"Tara, I know how to find out for sure if there's a coyote in the park!" she cried. "Come with me!"

CHAPTER 9

"Do you have an appointment?" asked the woman sitting behind the big desk.

"No," Berrie answered. She looked at Tara, who shrugged. She didn't know you had to have an appointment to see the park director, the way you did for the dentist.

"Well, Dr. Wheeler is very busy this week," said the woman. "He's presenting a paper at a conference tomorrow and after that . . ."

"But I just want to ask him about this strange animal I saw in the park," Berrie interrupted. "It shouldn't be there, but it is. I promise it will only take a little while."

The woman stood up. "I'll speak to Dr. Wheeler." She walked through a door behind the desk.

In less than a minute she was back, smiling. "Dr. Wheeler will talk to you. What is your name?"

"Berrie Lockwood."

"Berrie Lockwood, Dr. Wheeler," said the woman, holding the door open. Tara waited in her chair.

The desk in the office of the director of Crestwood Park was bigger than the one in the principal's office at school. It was covered with papers and books. A computer stood on one corner of the desk. Behind the desk was a man with a beard and glasses.

He stood up.

"Hello, Berrie. So I hear you've seen a strange animal in the park."

"Yes," said Berrie. "Two times. It was rainy and dark both times. And there wasn't anybody else around. I think that's why it came out."

"Tell me what it looked like," said Dr. Wheeler.

When Berrie had finished describing the animal, Dr. Wheeler went over to a bookcase on the wall. The bookcase was filled with books and went all the way to the ceiling. Dr. Wheeler took down a big book and opened it.

"Did it look like that?"

The picture looked *exactly* like the gray dog. Below it was something in a foreign language. *Canis Latrans.* "Yes!" said Berrie. "Can-is la-trans."

"That's the scientific name for the coyote," said Dr. Wheeler.

"It is a coyote!" said Berrie. "I knew it!"

"I've seen it myself. Once early in the morning and once at night. We've had coyotes in some of our city parks for the past year or so."

"But how did they get here?"

"Somebody might have brought some coyote pups to the city," said Dr. Wheeler. "When the pups grew up, their owner might

have let them go, or maybe they ran away. But I think the coyotes probably got here on their own. First they went to a park in one of the suburbs."

"And then their children went further in toward the city!" Berrie chimed in. "And one day a coyote came all the way to Crestwood Park."

"That's the way I think it happened," said Dr. Wheeler.

"I saw it grab a squirrel," said Berrie. She told Dr. Wheeler what she saw from the picnic shelter. "And the tail was hanging out of the coyote's mouth," she finished with a shudder.

"Coyotes eat rats and mice and rabbits, mostly," said Dr. Wheeler. "But they'll eat what they can get. Even pigeons."

Berrie made a face. Even pigeons! "We have to write about a wild animal for class," she said. "It has to be an animal we saw ourselves. I could write about coyotes, but now I don't like them. The squirrel was really cute."

"Coyotes need meat to live," said Dr. Wheeler. "Lots of animals eat other animals. They have to." He opened the drawer of his desk. "Here, I have something for you."

As she and Tara walked back through the park, Berrie looked at the typewritten pages Dr. Wheeler had given her. It was the speech he was going to give at the conference the next day. He was going to tell them about some of the strange animals that lived in Crestwood Park. One was the coyote. There was a fox, too. A fox! Maybe she'd see it someday!

They went out through the big wrought iron gates. The hot dog man was in front of the gates. Berrie sniffed. Hot dogs smelled so good! She loved hot dogs.

The coyote couldn't get hot dogs or fried chicken or hamburgers. But coyotes needed meat. So they had to eat mice and rats and rabbits—and squirrels. They couldn't live unless they ate things like that.

Berrie said good-bye to Tara at the corner. As she ran across the street, she thought about showing Mrs. Brindle what Dr. Wheeler said about the coyote in Crestwood Park. And then she would write about the coyote herself. She would win the prize, because all Jeff saw the bear do was cross the road.

CHAPTER 10

"There is a coyote living in Crestwood Park right now," said Berrie. "I saw it twice. But it only comes out when there aren't any people around. This coyote eats mice and rats and squirrels and rabbits. Coyotes have to eat food like that. It's the only way they can live."

The class was very quiet, staring at her. Jeff's mouth was open in surprise.

"I saw the coyote in Crestwood Park hunt a squirrel. First it stood very, very still, like a statue. It waited until the squirrel wasn't close to a tree. Then it ran after the squirrel. The coyote jumped up in the air. When it came down, its front paws grabbed the squirrel. When the coyote ran by me, I saw the squirrel's tail hanging out of the coyote's mouth."

Some of the kids made faces. But Jeff said a silent "Wow." Pleased by their reactions, Berrie went on. "Coyotes can live almost anyplace, even close to man. The Native Americans said the coyote would be the last animal on earth. I think they were right."

As she went back to her seat, the class clapped a long time. Tara smiled at her and nodded.

"Well!" said Mrs. Brindle as Berrie took her seat. "That was certainly a fascinating report, Berrie. Greg, what do you have to tell us about the mallard duck?"

Greg didn't have much to say about the mallard duck. Kelly had more to say about the raccoon. Then it was Jeff's turn. Berrie felt nervous as she watched Jeff march up the aisle carrying a box. What was in that box? she wondered.

Jeff stood next to Mrs. Brindle's desk. He took something out of the box. "This is a black bear tooth," he said, holding it up. "My uncle is a biologist, and he got this tooth from another biologist who studies bears."

Berrie felt a stab of jealousy. She didn't have a coyote tooth. What else was in the box?

Jeff talked about what big black bears were like, and how fast they ran, and where they lived. He didn't talk much about the bear he'd seen crossing the road. That was because he'd only seen it for a few seconds, thought Berrie. And all it did was cross the road. But then Jeff opened the box again. He took a piece of bear fur out of the box and passed it and the tooth around the room.

"My, that was very interesting, Jeff," said Mrs. Brindle. "And now, since Jeff was the last one to read his report, we're ready to vote on the best report."

Tara smiled back at Berrie. Yours, she mouthed.

Tara was a great friend, thought Berrie.

The class cast their votes on little slips of paper. They folded the slips and put them in a box on Mrs. Brindle's desk. When they were finished, Mrs. Brindle called Tara up to her desk. Tara took out the folded slips one by one and opened them. She read each name aloud. Mrs. Brindle made marks in her notebook. Tara put the slips in piles.

Berrie's heart beat fast every time Tara read her name. Soon there was a big pile of slips for Berrie. But Jeff's name was on lots of slips, too. His pile was as big as hers. Nobody else's pile was as big as their piles.

"That's all," said Tara.

"Hmmmm," said Mrs. Brindle, looking at her notebook. "It was a very close contest, but Jeff wins by one vote."

Jeff had won! Berrie slumped into her seat.

Smiling, Mrs. Brindle opened the bottom drawer of her desk. She took out a big package wrapped in brightly colored paper.

"Jeff, please come up to my desk."

Jeff unwrapped the package, then held it up for everyone to see. It was a big, thick book called *The Children's Encyclopedia of Animals*. Jeff opened the book, then held it up again. There were beautiful color pictures inside.

Berrie slumped lower into her seat. It would be nice to have *The Children's Encyclopedia of Animals*. She wouldn't have to go to the library so much. The book would be right there in her bookcase. She'd never spell an animal's name wrong again. She wondered what it said about coyotes.

After class, Tara said, "Yours was the best report. Jeff only won because he had the tooth and the fur."

"I guess," said Berrie. The tooth had been great. The hair, too. But all Jeff's bear did was cross the road. Her coyote did lots more.

They walked slowly along the sidewalk. Ahead of them, Berrie could see Jeff and Matt. Jeff carried the encyclopedia under his arm. Then he stopped and looked back.

"Hey, Berrie! Tara!" he called. The boys waited until the girls caught up with them.

"Did you really see the coyote grab the squirrel?" asked Jeff.

"Sure," said Berrie.

"Wow—that's something. I'd like to see that coyote. Do you think you could show it to me?"

"Maybe," said Berrie. "It takes a lot of patience, though."

"You know what, Berrie?" said Jeff. "I already have this book. My uncle the biologist gave it to me for my birthday. There's a picture of a coyote on this page." He gave her the open book.

The book was so heavy Berrie almost dropped it. The coyote in the picture had its head tipped way back. Its mouth was open. "Howling coyote," said the small print below the picture.

"I think yours was really the best animal," said Jeff. " After all, the bear I saw

was just running across the road. You can keep the book."

She looked from Jeff to Matt. Matt nodded in agreement. "Thanks!" she said.

The book felt as if it weighed a ton by the time she got it home. She read everything about the coyote. At dinner, her whole family admired the book.

"What gorgeous color photographs," said her mother.

"Can I borrow it sometime?" asked Jill.

"What kinds of information does it have?" asked her father.

"Facts," said Berrie. "Lots and lots of interesting facts!"

About the Author

Barbara Ford lives in New Jersey, where deer visit her yard, raccoons eat the food in the garden, hawks sit on the garage roof, and red foxes trot by in winter. A coyote hasn't shown up yet, but she expects to see one join the crowd soon. The author lives inside the house with her husband and their dog. Of course there *are* those funny noises overhead in the attic . . .

More great books from Troll

Louise the One and Only
by Elizabeth Koehler-Pentacoff
illustrated by R.W. Alley

The Peanut Butter Trap
by Elaine Moore
illustrated by Meredith Johnson

Wish Magic
by Elizabeth Koehler-Pentacoff
illustrated by R.W. Alley

Available wherever you buy books.

Louise
the One and Only

by
Elizabeth
Koehler-Pentacoff

illustrated by
R.W. Alley

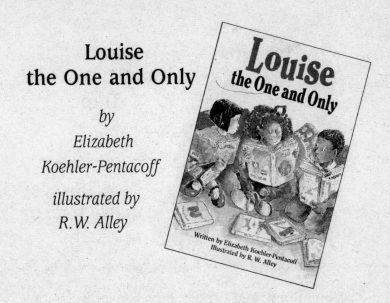

In this funny collection of stories, Louise and her classmates get into all sorts of crazy predicaments. Read how Louise convinces all her friends to change their names, which leaves Mr. Shelby, their teacher, very confused. Laugh along as Louise learns to swim, and helps put on a talent show. You'll soon discover that there's no one quite like Louise!

Available wherever you buy books.

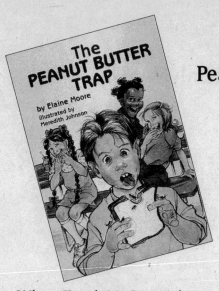

The Peanut Butter Trap

by
Elaine Moore

illustrated by
Meredith Johnson

When Frank McCormick puts icky grape bubble gum in Crystal's hair, she's had enough of his teasing and pranks. Together with her friends, Crystal cooks up the perfect revenge: a peanut butter-and-ant sandwich she tricks Frank into eating. But Frank doesn't react to the yucky sandwich the way Crystal expects him to. Instead, he comes up with a pretty gross plan of his own. Now Crystal is the one caught in *The Peanut Butter Trap!*

Available wherever you buy books.

Wish Magic

by
Elizabeth
Koehler-Pentacoff

illustrated by
R.W. Alley

Meg doesn't suspect a thing when her weird brother, Morris, gives her a powdered doughnut one morning. But right after she eats the doughnut, strange things start happening. Meg realizes that the breakfast treat has given her special powers—everything she wishes for comes true! Wish magic can be lots of fun, but it also brings Meg all kinds of problems. Will she ever be a regular kid again?

Available wherever you buy books.